COMIC ZONE

Disney's TALL TAILS

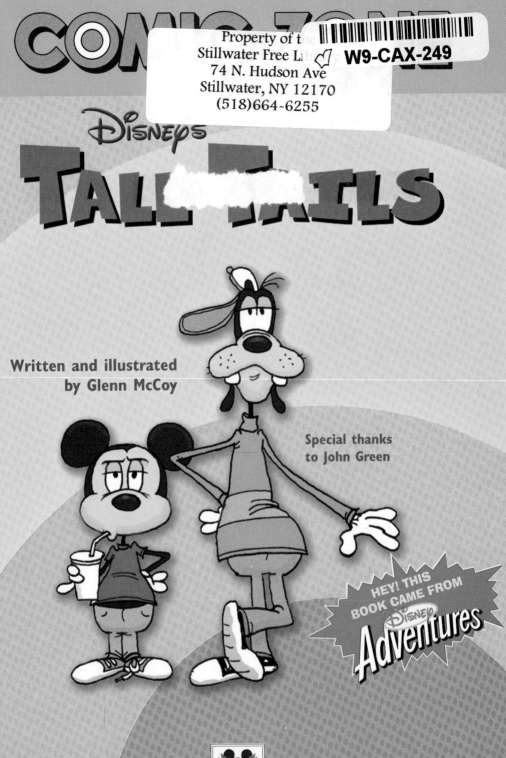

Written and illustrated
by Glenn McCoy

Special thanks
to John Green

HEY! THIS
BOOK CAME FROM
Disney
Adventures

Disney
PRESS

New York

Printed in the United States of America

First Edition

10 9 8 7 6 5 4 3 2 1

Library of Congress Catalog Card Number: 2005921322

ISBN 0-7868-3766-7

Visit www.disneybooks.com

Contents

Plus, many more!

"YOU SEW ME TOGETHER FROM TWENTY BODIES AND *THESE* ARE THE BEST EARS YOU COULD FIND?!"

DISNEY'S TALL TAILS HOT TUB

TALL TAILS   UFO-NO!

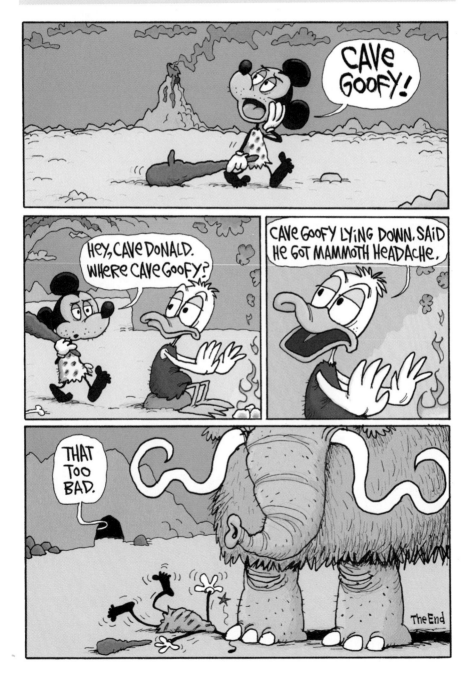

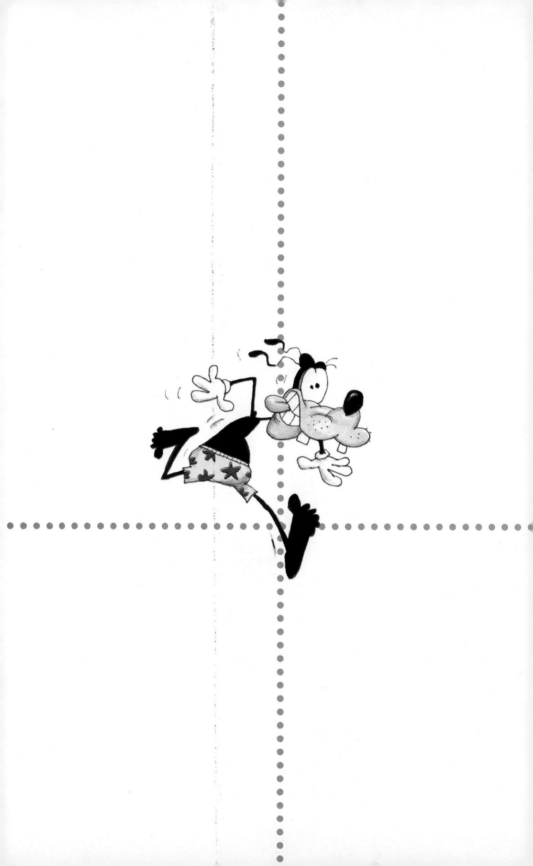

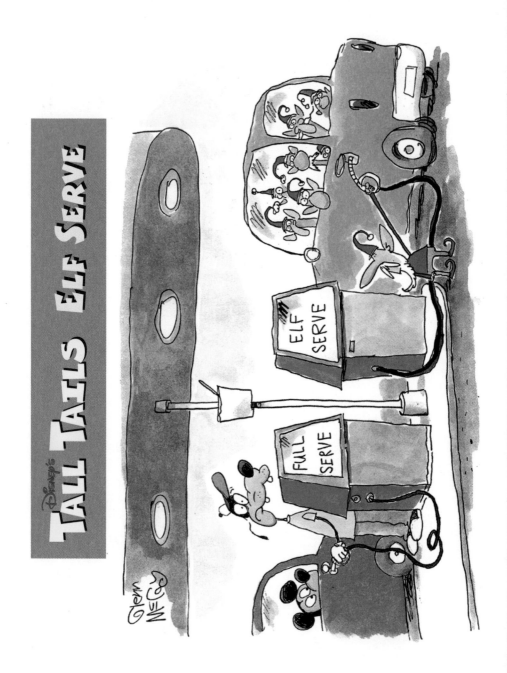

DISNEY'S TALL TAILS DENTAL CARE

MICKEY MOUSE?
HELLO. I'M —
HENRY HUMAN.

Disney's TALL TAILS CANNONBALL